Munschworks 3
The Third Munsch Treasury

Munschworks 3
The Third Munsch Treasury

stories by Robert Munsch and Michael Kusugak
illustrations by Michael Martchenko
and Vladyana Langer Krykorka

annick press
toronto • berkeley • vancouver

Munschworks 3 © 2000 Annick Press Ltd.
Cover art by Michael Martchenko.

Eleventh printing, January 2016

Stephanie's Ponytail
　　　　©1996 Bob Munsch Enterprises Ltd. (text)
　　　　©1996 Michael Martchenko (art)
Angela's Airplane
　　　　©1988 Bob Munsch Enterprises Ltd. (text)
　　　　©1988 Michael Martchenko (art)
Jonathan Cleaned Up—Then He Heard a Sound
　　　　©1981 Bob Munsch Enterprises Ltd. (text)
　　　　©1981 Michael Martchenko (art)
Show and Tell
　　　　©1991 Bob Munsch Enterprises Ltd. (text)
　　　　©1991 Michael Martchenko (art)
A Promise is a Promise
　　　　©1988 Bob Munsch Enterprises Ltd. (text)
　　　　©1988 Michael Kusugak (text)
　　　　©1988 Vladyana Krykorka (art)

Annick Press Ltd.

We acknowledge the support of the Canada Council for the Arts, the Ontario Arts Council,
and the Government of Canada through the Canada Book Fund (CBF) for our publishing activities.

ONTARIO ARTS COUNCIL
CONSEIL DES ARTS DE L'ONTARIO

an Ontario government agency
un organisme du gouvernement de l'Ontario

Cataloging in Publication Data

Munsch, Robert N., 1945-
　　　　Munschworks 3 : the third Munsch treasury

ISBN 1-55037-633-0

I. Martchenko, Michael. II. Krykorka, Vladyana. III. Title. IV. Title: Munschworks three.

PS8576.U575M86 2000　　　　jC813'.54　　　　C00-930199-2
PZ7.M927Mu 2000

The art in this book was rendered in watercolor.
The text was typeset in Century Oldstyle and Adlib.

Published in the U.S.A. by Annick Press (U.S.) Ltd.
Distributed in Canada by University of Toronto Press.
Distributed in the U.S.A. by Publishers Group West.

Printed and bound in China.

visit us at: **www.annickpress.com**
visit Robert Munsch at: **www.robertmunsch.com**

For e-book editions of many classic Robert Munsch stories, please visit annickpress.com/ebooks

Contents

Stephanie's Ponytail

by Robert Munsch
illustrated by
Michael Martchenko

One day Stephanie went to her mom and said, "None of the kids in my class have a ponytail. I want a nice ponytail coming right out the back."

So Stephanie's mom gave her a nice ponytail coming right out the back.

When Stephanie went to school, the other kids looked at her and said, "Ugly, ugly, very ugly."

Stephanie said, "It's *my ponytail* and *I* like it."

The next morning, when Stephanie went to school, all the other girls had ponytails coming out the back.

Stephanie looked at them and said, "You are all a bunch of copycats. You just do whatever I do. You don't have a brain in your heads."

The next morning the mom said, "Stephanie, would you like a ponytail coming out the back?"

Stephanie said, "No."

"Then that's that," said her mom. "That's the only place you can do ponytails."

"No, it's not," said Stephanie. "I want one coming out the side, just above my ear."

"Very strange," said the mom. "Are you sure that is what you want?"

"Yes," said Stephanie.

So her mom gave Stephanie a nice ponytail coming out right above her ear.

When she went to school, the other kids
saw her and said, "Ugly, ugly, very ugly."
Stephanie said, "It's *my ponytail* and *I* like it."
The next morning, when Stephanie came
to school, all the girls, and even some of the
boys, had nice ponytails coming out just above
their ears.

The next morning the mom said, "Stephanie, would you like a ponytail coming out the back?"

Stephanie said, "NNNO."

"Would you like one coming out the side?"

"NNNO!"

"Then that's that," said her mom. "There is no other place you can do ponytails."

"Yes, there is," said Stephanie. "I want one coming out of the top of my head like a tree."

"That's very, very strange," said her mom. "Are you sure that is what you want?"

"Yes," said Stephanie.

So her mom gave Stephanie a nice ponytail coming out of the top of her head like a tree. When Stephanie went to school, the other kids saw her and said, "Ugly, ugly, very ugly."

Stephanie said, "It's *my ponytail* and *I* like it."

The next day all of the girls and all of the boys had ponytails coming out the top. It looked like broccoli was growing out of their heads.

The next morning the mom said, "Stephanie, would you like a ponytail coming out the back?"

Stephanie said, "NNNO."

"Would you like one coming out the side?"

"NNNO!"

"Would you like one coming out the top?"

"*NNNO!*"

"Then that is definitely that," said the mom. "There is no other place you can do ponytails."

"Yes, there is," said Stephanie. "I want one coming out the front and hanging down in front of my nose."

"But nobody will know if you are coming or going," her mom said. "Are you sure that is what you want?"

"Yes," said Stephanie. So her mom gave Stephanie a nice ponytail coming out the front.

On the way to school she bumped into four trees, three cars, two houses and one Principal.

When she finally got to her class, the other kids saw her and said, "Ugly, ugly, very ugly."

Stephanie said, "It's *my ponytail* and *I* like it."

The next day all of the girls and all of the boys, and even the teacher, had ponytails coming out the front and hanging down in front of their noses. None of them could see where they were going. They bumped into the desks and they bumped into each other. They bumped into the walls and, by mistake, three girls went into the boys' bathroom.

Stephanie yelled, "You are a bunch of brainless copycats. You just do whatever I do. When I come tomorrow, I am going to have ... SHAVED MY HEAD!"

The first person to come the next day was the teacher. She had shaved her head and she was bald.

The next to come were the boys. They had shaved their heads and they were bald.

The next to come were the girls. They had shaved their heads and they were bald.

The last person to come was Stephanie, and she had ...

a nice little ponytail coming right out the back.

Angela's Airplane

by Robert Munsch
illustrated by
Michael Martchenko

Angela's father took her to the airport, but when they got there, a terrible thing happened: Angela's father got lost.

Angela looked under airplanes and on top of airplanes and beside airplanes, but she couldn't find him anyplace, so Angela decided to look *inside* an airplane.

She saw one with an open door and climbed up the steps: one, two, three, four, five, six—right to the top. Her father was not there, and neither was anyone else.

Angela had never been in an airplane before. In the front there was a seat that had lots of buttons all around it. Angela loved to push buttons, so she walked up to the front, sat down in the seat and said to herself, "It's okay if I push just *one* button. Don't you think it's okay if I push just *one* button? Oh yes, it's okay. Yes, yes, yes, yes."

Then she slowly pressed the bright red button. Right away the door closed.

Angela said, "It's okay if I push just one more button. Don't you think it's okay if I push just one more button? Oh yes, it's okay. Yes, yes, yes, yes." Slowly she pushed the yellow button. Right away the lights came on.

Angela said, "It's okay if I push just *one more* button. Don't you think it's okay if I push just *one more* button? Oh yes, it's okay. Yes, yes, yes, yes." She pushed the green button. Right away the motor came on: VROOM, VROOM, VROOM, VROOM.

Angela said, "Yikes," and pushed all the buttons at once. The airplane took off and went right up into the air.

When Angela looked out the window, she saw that she was very high in the sky. She didn't know how to get down. The only thing to do was to push one more button, so she slowly pushed the black button. It was the radio button. A voice came on the radio and said, "Bring back that airplane, you thief, you."

Angela said, "My name is Angela. I am five years old and I don't know how to fly airplanes."

"Oh dear," said the voice. "What a mess. Listen carefully, Angela. Take the steering wheel and turn it to the left."

Angela turned the wheel and very slowly the airplane went in a big circle and came back right over the airport.

"Okay," said the voice, "now pull back on the wheel."

Angela pulled back on the wheel and the airplane slowly went down to the runway. It hit once and bounced. It hit again and bounced. Then one wing scraped the ground. Right away the whole plane smashed and broke into little pieces.

Angela was left sitting on the ground and she didn't even have a scratch.

All sorts of cars and trucks came speeding out of the terminal.

There were police cars, ambulances, fire trucks and buses. And all sorts of people came running, but in front of everybody was Angela's father.

He picked her up and said, "Angela, are you all right?"

"Yes," said Angela.

"Oh, Angela," he said, "the airplane is not all right. It is in very small pieces."

"I know," said Angela, "it was a mistake."

"Well, Angela," said her father, "promise me you will never fly another airplane."

"I promise," said Angela.

"Are you sure?" said the father.

Angela said, very loudly, "I promise, I promise, I promise."

Angela didn't fly an airplane for a very long time. But when she grew up, she didn't become a doctor, she didn't become a truck driver, she didn't become a secretary and she didn't become a nurse. She became an airplane pilot.

Jonathan Cleaned Up—Then He Heard a Sound

by Robert Munsch

illustrated by Michael Martchenko

*J*onathan's mother went to get a can of noodles. She said, "Jonathan, please don't make a mess!"

When she was gone, Jonathan stood in the middle of the apartment and looked at the nice clean rug and the nice clean walls and the very, very clean sofa and said, "Well, there is certainly no mess here."

Then he heard a sound. It was coming from behind the wall. He put his ear up against the wall and listened very carefully.

The noise sounded like a train. Just then, the wall slid open and a subway train pulled up and stopped. Someone yelled, "LAST STOP! EVERYBODY OUT!" Then little people, big people, fat people and thin people, and all kinds of people, came out of Jonathan's wall, ran around his apartment and went out the front door.

Jonathan stood in the middle of the living room and looked around. There was writing on the wall, gum on the rug and a man sleeping on the sofa, and all the food was gone from the refrigerator.

"Well," said Jonathan, "this is certainly a mess!" Jonathan tried to drag the man out the door, but he met his mother coming in.

She saw the writing on the wall, the gum on the rug and the empty refrigerator. She yelled, "Jonathan, what a mess!"

Jonathan said, "The wall opened up and there was a subway train. Thousands of people came running through."

But his mother said, "Oh, Jon, don't be silly. Clean it up."

She went out to get another can of noodles, and Jonathan cleaned up. When he was all done, he heard a sound. It was coming from behind the wall. He put his ear up against the wall and listened very carefully. The noise sounded like a train. Someone yelled, "LAST STOP! EVERYBODY OUT!" And all kinds of people came out of Jonathan's wall, ran around his apartment and went out the front door.

This time there were ice cream cones and chewing gum on the rug, writing and foot-prints on the wall, two men sleeping on the sofa and a policeman watching TV. Besides that, the refrigerator was gone. Jonathan got angry and yelled, "Everybody out."

Just then his mother came in. She saw ice
cream cones and chewing gum on the rug,
writing and footprints on the wall, two men
sleeping on the sofa, a policeman watching TV
and a big empty space where the refrigerator
had been. "Jonathan," she said, "what have
you done?"

Then she heard a noise. It was coming from
behind the wall. She put her ear right against
the wall and listened very carefully. The noise
sounded like a train. Just then the wall slid
open and a subway train pulled up. Someone
yelled, "LAST STOP! EVERYBODY OUT!"
And all kinds of people ran out of Jonathan's
wall, ran around his apartment and went out
the front door.

There were ice cream cones, chewing gum and pretzel bags on the rug, writing and footprints and handprints on the wall, and five men sleeping on the sofa. Besides that, a policeman and a conductor were watching TV, and the fridge and stove were gone.

Jonathan went to the conductor and said, "This is not a subway station, this is my house!"

The conductor said, "If the subway stops here, then it's a subway station! You shouldn't build your house in a subway station. If you don't like it, go see City Hall."

So Jonathan went to City Hall.

When he got there, the lady at the front desk told him to see the subway boss, and the subway boss told Jonathan to go see the Mayor.

So he went and saw the Mayor. The Mayor said, "If the subway stops there, then it's a subway station! You shouldn't build your house in a subway station. Our computer says it's a subway station, and our computer is never wrong." Then he ran out for lunch.

In fact, everyone ran out for lunch, and
Jonathan was all by himself at City Hall.
Jonathan started to leave, but on his way out
he heard a sound.

Someone was crying, "Oooooooh, I'm hungry." Jonathan listened very carefully. He walked up and down the hall and found the room it was coming from. He went in, and there was a big, enormous, shining computer machine. The computer was going "wing, wing, kler-klung, clickety clang," and its lights were going off and on. The voice was coming from behind it.

Jonathan squeezed in back of the machine and saw a little old man at a very messy desk. The man looked at Jonathan and said, "Do you have any blackberry jam?"

"No," said Jonathan, "but I could get you some. Who are you?"

"I'm the computer," said the man.

Now, Jonathan was no dummy. He said, "Computers are machines, and you are not a machine. They go 'wing, wing, kler-klung, clickety clang.'"

The man pointed at the big computer and said, "Well, that goes 'wing, wing, kler-klung, clickety clang,' but the darn thing never did work. I do everything for the whole city."

"Oh," said Jonathan. "I will get you some blackberry jam if you'll do me a favor. A subway station is in my house at 980 Young Street. Please change it."

"Certainly," said the old man. "I remember doing that. I didn't know where to put it."

Jonathan ran out and passed all the offices with nobody there. He ran down the stairs and all the way to a jam store. He got four cases of jam. It took him three hours to carry it all the way back to City Hall. There was still nobody there. He carried the jam back behind the computer and put it on the floor.

"Now," said the old man, "where am I going to put this subway station?"

"I know," said Jonathan, and he whispered in the old man's ear. Then he left. But the old man yelled after him, "Don't tell anyone the computer is broken. The Mayor would be very upset. He paid ten million dollars for it."

When Jonathan got home, his mother was still standing on the rug, because she was stuck to the gum.

Jonathan started washing the writing off the wall. He said, "There will be no more subways here."

And he was right.

Show and Tell

by Robert Munsch
illustrated by
Michael Martchenko

*B*enjamin wanted to take something really neat to school for show and tell, so he decided to take his new baby sister. He went upstairs, picked her up, put her in his knapsack and walked off to school.

But when Ben sat down, his baby sister finally woke up. She was not happy inside the knapsack and started to cry: "WAAA, WAAA, WAAA, WAAA, WAAA."

The teacher looked at him and said, "Benjamin, stop making that noise."

Ben said, "That's not me. It's my baby sister. She's in my knapsack. I brought her for show and tell."

"Yikes!" said the teacher. "You can't keep a baby in a knapsack!" She grabbed Ben's knapsack and opened it up. The baby looked at the teacher and said, "WAAA, WAAA, WAAA, WAAA, WAAA."

"Don't worry," said the teacher. "I know how to take care of babies." She picked it up and rocked it back and forth, back and forth, back and forth.

Unfortunately, the teacher was not the baby's mother and she didn't rock quite right. The baby cried even louder: "WAAA, WAAA, WAAA, WAAA, WAAA."

The principal came running in. He looked at the teacher and said, "Stop making that noise!"

The teacher said, "It's not me. It's Sharon, Ben's new baby sister. He brought her for show and tell. She won't shut up!"

The principal said, "Ah, don't worry. I know how to make kids be quiet." He picked up the baby and yelled, "HEY, YOU! BE QUIET!" The baby did not like that at all. It screamed, really loudly, "WAAA, WAAA, WAAA, WAAA, WAAA."

The principal said, "What's the matter with this baby? It must be sick. I'll call a doctor."

The doctor came with a big black bag. She looked in the baby's eyes and she looked in the baby's ears and she looked in the baby's mouth. She said, "Ah! Don't worry. I know what to do. This baby needs a needle!"

So the doctor opened her bag, got out a short needle and said, "Naaaah, TOO SMALL."

The doctor opened her bag, got out a longer needle and said, "Naaaah, TOO SMALL."

The doctor opened her bag, got out a really long needle and said, "Naaaah, TOO SMALL."

The doctor reached into her bag, got out an enormous needle and said, "Ahhh, JUST RIGHT."

When the baby saw that enormous needle, it yelled, as loudly as it could, "WAAA, WAAA, WAAA, WAAA, WAAA."

Ben said, "What's the matter with this school? Nobody knows what to do with a baby." He ran down to the principal's office and called his mother on the phone. He said, "HELP, HELP, HELP! You have to come to school right away."

The mother said, "Ben, your little sister is lost! I can't come to school. I have to find her."

"She's not lost," said Ben. "I took her to school in my knapsack."

"Oh, no!" yelled the mother. She ran down the street and into the school. The principal and the teacher and the doctor were standing around the baby, and the baby was yelling, as loudly as possible, "WAAA, WAAA, WAAA, WAAA, WAAA."

The mother picked up the baby
and rocked it back and forth,
back and forth, back and forth.
The baby said, "Ahhhhhhhh,"
and went to sleep.

"Oh, thank you! Oh, thank you!" said the principal. "That baby was making so much noise, it was just making me feel sick!"

"SICK?" said the doctor. "SICK! Did that man say he was SICK? He must need a needle." So the doctor opened her bag, got out a short needle and said, "Naaaah, TOO SMALL."

The doctor opened her bag, got out a longer needle and said, "Naaaah, TOO SMALL."

The doctor opened her bag, got out a really long needle and said, "Naaaah, TOO SMALL."

The doctor reached into her bag, got out an enormous needle and said, "Ahhh, JUST RIGHT."

The principal looked at that enormous needle and said, "WAAA, WAAA, WAAA, WAAA, WAAA," and ran out the door.

"Now," said the mother, "it's time to take this baby home."

"Right," said Ben. "You can use my knapsack."

"What a good idea," said the mother.

Ben and his mother put the baby into bed.
She went to sleep and didn't cry, not even once.

Ben went back to school carrying some strange things for show and tell.

And he wasn't out of place at all ...

A Promise is a Promise

by Robert Munsch and Michael Kusugak
illustrated by Vladyana Krykorka

On the very first nice day of spring Allashua said, "I'm going to go fishing. I'm going to go fishing in the ocean. I'm going to go fishing in the cracks in the ice."

"Ah, ah," said her mother, "don't go fishing on the sea ice. Under the sea ice live Qallu-pilluit. They grab children who aren't with their parents. Don't go fishing in the ocean. Go fish in a lake."

"Right," said Allashua. "I promise to go fishing in the lake and not in the ocean, and a promise is a promise."

So Allashua set out like she was going to go to the lake near her house, but when she got to the end of the street, she didn't go to the lake. She walked down the long snowy path that led to the ocean.

At the edge of the ocean were large cracks where the tide broke and jumbled the ice. Allashua looked very carefully and did not see any Qallupilluit. She said, "On TV I have seen Santa Claus, Fairy Godmothers and the Tooth Fairy, but never any Qallupilluit. I think my mother is wrong."

But just in case her mother was right, Allashua stood beside the sea ice and yelled, "Qallupilluit have dirty noses."

Nothing happened.

Allashua yelled, "Qallupilluit smell like a dead whale in the summer."

Nothing happened.

Allashua walked right out onto the sea ice and yelled, as loud as she could, "Qallupilluit, Qallupilluit can't catch me!"

Nothing happened. The only thing Allashua heard was the sound of snow blowing over the ice.

So Allashua got out her line and her hook. She walked over to a large crack in the ice and started to fish. Right away a fish grabbed the hook and Allashua pulled it up. She caught six fish in a row.

Allashua yelled, "I am the best fisherman in the world!"

And from behind her something said, with a voice that sounded like snow blowing over the ice, *"The best you may be, but the smartest you are not."*

Allashua turned around. There, between her and the shore, were the Qallupilluit. They looked at her and said, *"Have you seen the child who said Qallupilluit have dirty noses?"*

"Oh, no, Qallupilluit. I have seen no such child, and besides, your noses are very pretty."

"Have you seen the child who said we smell like a dead whale in the summertime?"

"Oh, no, Qallupilluit. I have seen no such child, and besides, you smell very nice, just like flowers in the summer."

"Have you seen the child who yelled, 'Qallupilluit, Qallupilluit can't catch me'?"

"Oh, no, Qallupilluit. I have seen no such child, and besides, my mother says that you can catch whatever you want to."

"Right," said the Qallupilluit. *"We catch whatever we want to, and what we want to catch right now is you."*

One grabbed Allashua by her feet and dragged her down, down, under the sea ice to where the Qallupilluit live.

The sea water stung Allashua's face like fire. Allashua held her breath and the Qallupilluit gathered around her and sang, with voices that sounded like snow blowing over the ice:

> *Human child, human child*
> *Ours to have, ours to hold.*
> *Forget your mother, forget your father;*
> *Ours to hold under the ice.*

Allashua let out her breath and yelled, "My brothers and sisters, my brothers and sisters; I'll bring them all to the sea ice."

For a moment nothing happened, and then the Qallupilluit threw Allashua up out of the sea into the cold wind of the ice and said, *"A promise is a promise. Bring your brothers and sisters to the sea ice and we will let you go."*

Allashua began to run up the long, snow-covered path that led to her home. As she ran, her clothes started to freeze. She ran more and more slowly, until she fell to the ground. And that is where Allashua's father found her, almost at the back door, frozen to the snow.

Allashua's father gave a great yell, picked up Allashua and carried her inside. He tore off Allashua's icy clothes and put her to bed. Then the father and mother got under the covers and hugged Allashua till she got warm.

After an hour Allashua asked for some hot tea. She drank ten cups of hot tea with lots of sugar and said, "I went to the cracks in the sea ice."

"Ah, ah," said her family, "not so smart."

"I called the Qallupilluit nasty names."

"Ah, ah," said her family, "dumber still."

"I promised to take my brothers and sisters to the cracks in the sea ice. I promised to take them all to the Qallupilluit."

"Ah, ah," said her family, "a promise is a promise." Then her mother and father made some tea and they sat and drank it, and didn't say anything for a long time.

From far down the snow-covered path that led to the sea, the Qallupilluit began calling, *"A promise is a promise. A promise is a promise. A promise is a promise."*

The mother looked at her children and said, "I have an idea. Do exactly as I say. When I start dancing, all of you follow Allashua to the cracks in the sea ice."

And the children all whispered to each other, "Ah, ah, why will our mother dance? This is not a happy time."

Allashua's mother went out the back door and yelled, "Qallupilluit, Qallupilluit, come and talk with me."

And they did come, right up out of the cracks in the sea ice. Up the long, snow-covered path to the sea they came, and stood by the back door. It was a most strange thing, for never before had the Qallupilluit left the ocean.

The mother and father cried and yelled and asked for their children back, but the Qallupilluit said, "A promise is a promise."

The mother and father begged and pleaded and asked for their children back, but the Qallupilluit said, "A promise is a promise."

Finally Allashua's mother said, "Qallupilluit, you have hearts of ice; but a promise is a promise. Come and join us while we say good-bye to our children."

Everyone went inside. First the mother gave her children some bread. She said to the Qallupilluit, "This is not for you." But the Qallupilluit said, *"We want some too."* The mother gave the Qallupilluit some bread, and they liked it a lot.

Then the mother gave each of her children a piece of candy. She said to the Qallupilluit, "This is not for you." But the Qallupilluit said, *"We want some too."* The mother gave the Qallupilluit some candy, and they liked it a lot.

130

Then the father started to dance. He said to the Qallupilluit, "This is not for you." The Qallupilluit said, "We have never danced. We want to dance." And they all started to dance. First they danced slowly and then they danced fast, and then they started to jump and yell and scream and dance a wild dance. The Qallupilluit liked the dancing so much that they forgot about children.

Finally the mother started to dance, and when the children saw their mother dancing, they crawled out the back door and ran down the long, snowy path that led to the sea. They came to the cracks in the sea ice and Allashua whispered, "Qallupilluit, Qallupilluit, here we are."

Nothing happened.

Then all the children said, "Qallupilluit, Qallupilluit, here we are."

Nothing happened.

Then all the children yelled, as loud as they could, "Qallupilluit, Qallupilluit, here we are!"

Nothing happened, and they all went back to the land and sat on a large rock by the beach.

Two minutes later the Qallupilluit ran screaming down the path and jumped into their cracks in the ice. Allashua stood up on the rock and said, "A promise is what you were given and a promise is what you got. I brought my brothers and sisters to the sea ice, but you were not here. A promise is a promise."

The Qallupilluit yelled and screamed and pounded the ice till it broke. They begged and pleaded and asked to have the children, but Allashua said, "A promise is a promise." Then the Qallupilluit jumped down to the bottom of the sea and took their cracks with them, and the whole ocean of ice became perfectly smooth.

Then the mother and father came walking down the long, snowy path to the ocean. They hugged and kissed each one of their children, even Allashua. The father looked at the flat ocean and said, "We will go fishing here, for Qallupilluit have promised never to catch children with their parents, and a promise is a promise."

Then they all did go fishing, quite happily. Except for Allashua. She had been too close to the Qallupilluit and could still hear them singing, with voices that sounded like blowing snow:

> *Human child, human child*
> *Ours to have, ours to hold.*
> *Forget your mother, forget your brother;*
> *Ours to hold under the ice.*

A Qallupilluq is an imaginary Inuit creature, somewhat like a troll, that lives in Hudson Bay. It wears a woman's parka made of loon feathers and reportedly grabs children when they come too near cracks in the ice.

The Inuit traditionally spend a lot of time on the sea ice, so the Qallupilluit were clearly invented as a means to help keep small children away from dangerous crevices.

Michael Kusugak, thinking back to his childhood in the Arctic, made up a story about his own encounter with the Qallupilluit. He sent it to Robert Munsch, who had stayed with Michael's family while telling stories in Rankin Inlet, N.W.T. *A Promise is a Promise* is a result of their collaboration.

The Munsch for Kids series:

The Dark
Mud Puddle
The Paper Bag Princess
The Boy in the Drawer
Jonathan Cleaned Up, Then He Heard a Sound
Murmel Murmel Murmel
Millicent and the Wind
Mortimer
The Fire Station
Angela's Airplane
David's Father
Thomas' Snowsuit
50 Below Zero
I Have to Go!
Moira's Birthday
A Promise is a Promise
Pigs
Something Good
Show and Tell
Purple, Green and Yellow
Wait and See
Where is Gah-Ning?
From Far Away
Stephanie's Ponytail

Munschworks: The First Munsch Collection
Munschworks 2: The Second Munsch Treasury
Munschworks 4: The Fourth Munsch Treasury
The Munschworks Grand Treasury
Munsch Mini-Treasury One
Munsch Mini-Treasury Two
Munsch Mini-Treasury Three

For information on these titles please visit www.annickpress.com.
Many Munsch titles are available in French and/or Spanish, as well as in
board book and e-book editions. Please contact your favorite supplier.

How much Munsch have YOU read?

    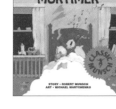

Collections:

Drama: **Board Books:**

Have you read them all?